The New Best Friend

1 Here Comes the Bride

2 Little Treasures

3 Fancy Dress Ponies

4 Pony Club Weekend

5 The New Best Friend

6 Ponies to the Rescue

www.**kids**at**randomhouse**.co.uk

For fun, games and lots, lots more visit
www.**katiesperfectponies**.co.uk

For Katie Price's adult website visit
www.**katieprice**.co.uk

THE NEW BEST FRIEND
A BANTAM BOOK 978 0 553 82072 0

First published in Great Britain by Bantam,
an imprint of Random House Children's Books
A Random House Group Company

This edition published 2007

1 3 5 7 9 10 8 6 4 2

Set in 14/21pt Bembo MT Schoolbook

Bantam Books are published by Random House Children's Books,
61–63 Uxbridge Road, London W5 5SA

www.**kids**at**randomhouse**.co.uk
www.rbooks.co.uk

Addresses for companies within The Random House Group Limited
can be found at: www.randomhouse.co.uk/offices.htm

THE RANDOM HOUSE GROUP Limited Reg. No. 954009
A CIP catalogue record for this book is available from the British Library.

Printed in the UK by CPI Bookmarque, Croydon, CR0 4TD

The New Best Friend

Illustrated by Dynamo Design

Bantam Books

Vicki's Riding School

Vicki

Jess and Rose

Cara and Taffy

Amber and Stella

Sam and Beanz

Mel and Candy

Henrietta and President

Darcy and Duke

Chapter 1

Holding a newspaper in one hand and her lunch box in the other, Amber ran up the drive to Vicki's Riding School with an excited grin on her face. There were tons of golden leaves piled up along the drive. Amber kicked

some high up into the air, then laughed as they swirled down and landed in her long, jet-black hair. She couldn't wait to tell her friends about the sponsored ride her mum had spotted in the paper the day before.

1

It was so cool when the girls could do special events together. It meant they got to spend even more time with each other, and with their ponies too! The pony club weekend in the summer holidays had been wicked and the treasure hunt they'd done in the spring had been brilliant too. Amber and her friend Jess had won the event and raised loads of money for charity.

Amber spotted Sam at the top of the drive. She was messing around in the leaves too and had a few stuck in her spiky ginger hair.

"Hiya!" Sam called out, smiling as usual.

Amber legged it up the drive to catch up with her.

Sam pointed at the newspaper under her arm and grinned. "Have you got a part-time job as a paper girl now?" she joked.

"No, stupid!" Amber replied. "But there's something in here I want you all to look at," and she smiled mysteriously at her friend.

Sam tried to grab the paper but Amber shook her head.

"No! I'll show you when we're all together," she said firmly. "I haven't even told Jess yet."

Jess was Amber's best friend at the stables. They did everything together. They usually walked to the stables together too, but Jess hadn't been at home when Amber had called for her this morning.

Sam looked excited. "You haven't told Jess yet? Wicked! I love surprises. I hope everyone else gets a move on so we can hear what it is."

★

Amber and her friends at the stables were
a close group of girls. They were all totally
different, but Amber thought that was
probably why they got on so well. Even this
early in the morning, freckly Sam bubbled
with jokes and confidence. Their friend Cara,
with her long blonde hair, was the total
opposite though; she was shy, quiet and very
nervous of new things and people. Skinny Mel
had dark curly hair, soft brown skin and big
dark eyes, she was the best rider and jumper
of all the girls. Then, of course, there was
Jess. She was really pretty,
with stunning green eyes
and thick brown hair.
The girls often looked to
Jess to tell them what to
do, and she and clever,
sensitive Amber made
a great team.

Even though they were all so different, the girls had one big thing in common: they were mad about ponies.

Amber, Jess, Mel, Sam and Cara loved helping with all the jobs that needed doing round the yard. Grooming the ponies, mucking out the stables, cleaning the tack, hosing down the yard, even tidying the muck heap – it was all fun when you loved ponies as much as they did! In return for their hard work Vicki gave them a free riding lesson every week as well as the one their parents managed to scrape the money together for. When they'd proved how reliable they all were, she'd given each girl a pony to look after as if it was her own. Vicki had told all the girls that their new responsibility would mean a lot of hard work. But it was the sort of hard work they couldn't get enough of!

The girls idolized Vicki. She was a brilliant rider and still won loads of competitions with

Jelly, her fabulous Irish-cross thoroughbred.
With her slim figure, thick dark hair and
tanned skin, she was also proof that you
could still look gorgeous and be a brilliant
horsewoman.

When Vicki had told Amber that she could
look after Stella, the lovely black Highland
pony, she had nearly fainted with happiness!
She'd fallen in love with Stella the moment
she set eyes on her. They suited each other
perfectly. They were both steady and calm
and always seemed to know what the other
one was thinking. Amber loved
grooming Stella's black coat
until it shone, and Sam
always teased her
when she saw her
cuddling her pony.
"You two are
like twins!" she
joked.

Sam looked after frisky Beanz, a skewbald
New Forest cross with a mind of his own.
Sam and Beanz were made for each other too.
Both of them were high-spirited and had bags
of energy.

Mel was a tough and fearless jumper: she
needed to be to handle the pony she was
in charge of – Candice, a lively Arab who
everybody called Candy. She was a beautiful
chestnut mare who could gallop like the wind,
and even that wasn't fast enough for Mel, who
always loved a challenge!

Cara, the smallest of the girls, rode Taffy, a
little palomino Welsh who wouldn't hurt a fly.
Getting to know laid-back Taffy had changed
Cara's life: he had given her the confidence to
learn to ride, and now she was even jumping!

Jess was responsible for Rose, a graceful
and good-natured grey Connemara pony.
Rose and Stella had stables next door to
each other, which is how Jess and Amber had

become best friends. When Amber couldn't get to the stables to muck out Stella, Jess would do it for her, and vice versa. Both girls knew they could totally trust the other to help out with their pony if need be.

There were other girls at the stables too, but they owned their ponies, which they kept at livery there. Amber and the other yard girls had made friends with one of the livery girls, Darcy. Darcy was a nice girl with a long dark plait that dangled down her back and ended just below her bottom. She was loads of fun and she loved the ponies as much as Amber and her friends did. She owned Duke, a beautiful dark bay show-jumper who had a stable full of rosettes from competitions they'd won together.

Darcy wasn't like the other snooty livery girls. She went to a posh school like they did, and the girls could tell that her parents were quite well off, but she was different. Darcy enjoyed having a laugh with the yard girls, and when she had time, she always looked after Duke herself – mucking out his stable, mixing his feeds, filling his hay-net – because she loved him so much.

Henrietta Reece-Thomas and Camilla Worthington, two of the other livery girls, couldn't have been more different. They would never bother to muck out their pony's stable or pick out its feet! Their parents paid Vicki to do that, and if there was anything at all they weren't happy with, they complained immediately. Amber and the other yard girls had a weekly livery rota, which meant that two of them were always responsible for feeding, grooming and mucking out the livery ponies.

Henrietta's pony was President, a stunning spotty grey Appaloosa. Amber passed President's stable on her way to say good morning to Stella. "Hi, handsome," she called softly to the lovely pony.

At the sound of her voice, he whinnied
and moved towards her. Henrietta's wealthy
parents had bought President as a surprise
present for their only daughter. For all the
money that was thrown at him though,
Amber always felt sorry for him. She'd never
seen Henrietta cuddle or talk to him. Amber
did it all the time when Henrietta wasn't

around because she knew how much he wanted somebody to love him.

Henrietta's best friend, Camilla Worthington, owned Cleopatra, a scary Arab pony from racehorse stock with a very bad temper. Everybody except Vicki was a little bit scared of Cleo, even Camilla!

Sam's voice calling from across the yard brought Amber out of her thoughts.

"Come on, Amber!" she yelled impatiently. "Everyone's here. We want our surprise!"

Amber patted President's soft silky neck. "Mel and Cara'll be back soon to muck you out, sweetheart," she said as she turned and, still holding the newspaper, ran across the yard to find her friends.

She followed Sam over to the tack room and smiled to herself. She could hear the girls chatting even from quite far away! At first they were talking so loudly that they didn't notice Amber and Sam come in.

"So then, after the sleepover, Lauren's mum dropped me here this morning," Jess was saying. "Lauren loved the ponies. She's *so* cool, you know."

Amber felt a funny feeling in her belly, and all of a sudden she wasn't in such a good mood. For about a month now Lauren, a girl Jess knew from school, had been mentioned more and more. From the way Jess described her she sounded gorgeous – popular and really cool. Amber had started to worry a little bit that Jess might not want to hang around with her any more when she could have Lauren.

"Right," Sam shouted, interrupting the conversation. "Amber's here now. Time for her surprise."

Amber didn't feel like telling them now, and she noticed that Jess didn't even look that interested. She forced herself to smile though, and opened the paper to the page she wanted before spreading it out on the tack-room table. All the girls gathered round to read a big advert in bold black type.

"A sponsored ride!" Mel yelled excitedly.

Amber nodded. "It's a fundraising event for that same special needs school that we did the treasure hunt for," she said. "They're trying to make enough money to get a little farm for the school."

As if they'd heard their names, two frisky puppies came scampering into the tack room, barking excitedly. Cara smiled and bent to pick them up. "Treasure and Hunt!" she cried.

The cute little puppies belonged to Vicki, who had named them after the treasure hunt the girls had done in the spring. Halfway round the course Cara and Mel had found the puppies drowning in a millpond. They'd rescued them and brought them back to the stables, where Vicki fell in love with them straight away.

"Cool!" said Jess, looking interested now. "What do we have to do?"

Amber smiled and read from the paper: "You get sponsors to give you money for every jump you do, so if you got sponsored for a pound a jump and you did twenty jumps you'd make twenty pounds for the school."

Cara, who had stopped cuddling Treasure and Hunt, looked at Jess and Amber in horror. "Twenty jumps!" she squeaked.

Sam ruffled her long blonde hair. "Don't stress, Car. You don't have to jump the ones you don't like the look of," she said. Then she grinned. "So we're up for it then?"

Even Cara couldn't help getting excited when enthusiastic Sam was around! "OK, I'm in!" she said.

"Yay! Good one, Car," said Mel. "Let's ask Vicki if it's OK this afternoon when the lessons are done."

Amber looked at her watch. "Hey, guys," she said, holding it out for them to see. "We need to get a move on – lessons will be starting soon and we haven't done anything yet."

They all jumped up quickly and ran to start tacking up their ponies.

"Is that a new watch, Amber?" Jess asked as they approached Rose and Stella's stables. "Lauren's got one just like it. It's well nice."

The funny feeling in Amber's belly came back and she felt a bit like crying. She looked at the floor, then busied herself tacking up Stella.

★

Saturdays were always really hectic and the lessons went quickly. It felt like no time before they were over and Amber was walking Stella back to her stable to untack her and brush her down. She noticed Jess stay behind to chat to Vicki and thought she might be talking to her about the sponsored ride. Amber smiled to herself. Maybe she was just over-reacting about Jess and her new friend. All the girls chatted, sometimes about people they knew from school. What did it matter if

Jess had stayed over at Lauren's house?

But when Jess came back, Amber's mood
changed quickly.

"I'm *so* excited, Amber!" she said. "I told
Vicki that Lauren loved the ponies and she
says it's fine for Lauren to come next week
and decide if she wants to start riding. Isn't
that cool?!" Jess had a big smile on her face.
"You'll really like her, Am. She's brilliant."

Amber forced herself to smile for Jess's sake.
She and Jess had always been best friends at
the stables. But Amber couldn't help thinking
things would be different with Lauren
around.

Chapter 2

The next Saturday Amber called for Jess as usual but she wasn't there again. "She left half an hour ago with Lauren, love," said Jess's mum. "I thought you knew."

Amber tried not to look upset and set off by herself. When she arrived at the stables, her friends were sitting around chatting in the tack room as they had been the week before. But this time Amber noticed straight away that there was an extra person there. Lauren!

She was amazed when she saw her. Lauren was their age but she looked a lot older. She had short, dark brown hair that had been cleverly cut so that it feathered round her

face and it had been highlighted with silver-
blonde streaks. Amber was shocked. Her
mum wouldn't let her dye her hair until she
was at least sixteen! Lauren wore sparkly
earrings and she had a silver ring on nearly
every finger, and her thumbs too! Her eyes
were hazel with green bits, her nose was cute
and upturned and she had a wide smiling
mouth and dazzling white teeth. Amber
could see why Jess liked her – she looked like
a film star and she laughed a lot.

Lauren was full of confidence too, by the
looks of it. She was sitting happily chatting
to the yard girls as if she'd known them for
ages. Amber remembered her own first day
– she'd been scared stiff, but Lauren didn't
look bothered at all.

"I'm sure I'll pick up how to ride easily,"
Lauren said confidently.

Cara, who was a bit shocked by her,
looked worried. "Riding can be a bit tricky

the first time," she said quietly. "It's taken me a while to learn properly so don't worry if you can't do everything first time."

Lauren tossed her pretty hair and grinned. "Stuff like this doesn't bother me," she replied. "I'm a really quick learner."

Amber felt uncomfortable around Lauren straight away but she tried not to show it. "Hi, you must be Lauren," she said, coming closer. "I'm Amber. I bet Jess has talked about me."

Lauren scratched her head and looked a bit puzzled. "Amber?" she said. "No, I don't think Jess has mentioned you."

All the others, except Jess, instantly saw Amber's face fall.

"I'm sure I must have, Lauren," said Jess. "Amber's pony's in the stable next to mine." And that was it. Nothing about them being best friends for ages, walking to the yard together, winning the treasure hunt together.

"No worries," said Amber, trying not to show she was upset. "Anyway, we're on livery duty from today, Jess. We'd better get started."

"Sorry, babe," said Jess in a high, girly voice that wasn't like her normal one at all, "but I won't be able to do the livery ponies this morning. I've got to show Lauren round and I promised her she could tack up Rose."

Amber was really annoyed with Jess: mucking out three stables on a busy Saturday morning was a lot to ask, and she was really surprised that Jess was going to let Lauren tack up Rose. She knew Stella would hate it if a total stranger who knew nothing about ponies walked into her stable and started tacking her up. Amber felt like crying, but there was no way she was going to look like a baby in front of Lauren. She held back her tears but, because she was worried about Rose, she asked, "Have you asked Vicki if that's OK?"

Jess shrugged and walked towards the tack-room door with Lauren.

"Vicki won't mind," she said confidently.

So Amber went over to President's and Cleopatra's stables and mucked them out; then she fed them and brushed them both down. Amber was normally the most sensitive to the ponies' needs, but she was so busy and upset that she didn't concentrate properly and got a bite from Cleo. After she had turned them out to graze in the pony meadow, Amber ran back to Stella's stable, where she did the whole thing all over again. Feeling hot and flustered, she tacked up Stella for Saturday lessons and walked her over to the indoor school, where the young riders were already noisily gathered, waiting to start.

Vicki never put up with any messing about and liked to start on time. As soon as she saw Amber, she called out, "Come on, Amber – what kept you?"

Before Amber could explain, Vicki clapped

her hands and shouted to the young riders,
"Trot in a circle please."

The confident riders rode by themselves
but the new or younger ones were always
led by one of the yard girls. Holding onto
Stella's lead rope, Amber jogged round the
school with a little girl called Becky on the
pony's back. Out of the corner of her eye she
could see Lauren
standing at the
side watching
them. But the
next time she
looked up, Amber
saw that Lauren
was leading
little Ben
round on Rose
and Jess was
just standing
watching.

It was clear that Rose didn't like the swap and neither did Ben. Rose tossed her head as Lauren tugged and pulled on her reins. The pony was so agitated she nearly bucked Ben off: he was hanging on desperately and looking round for somebody to help him. Amber was just about to go over when Vicki noticed what was happening and frowned.

"Will you do your job and lead Rose, Jess?" she shouted sharply. As Jess took the lead rope, Lauren scowled across at Vicki, then sat down with her arms folded grumpily.

Sam, who was leading Beanz behind Amber, muttered, "Oooh, touchy!" and both the girls giggled.

Lessons carried on as normal after that. Saturday mornings were always really busy. As one class arrived, another one left, and often there were tears as the young riders had to leave their favourite ponies. It was only at twelve thirty that there was peace and quiet in the yard again.

By then the ponies were tired, and the

girls were too! The ponies were all ready to be untacked and turned out into the pony meadow, where they could chill out for the rest of the afternoon. As Amber and her friends were untacking their ponies, Lauren came walking up.

"Hey, Jess, you said I could ride Rose today and I still haven't," she said.

Amber looked up to see what her friend would do.

Jess looked uncomfortable. "Rose has had a busy morning – she's tired," she replied. "Let her have a little rest and maybe you could have a ride this afternoon."

Lauren looked a bit put out. "But you *promised*," she whined. "I let you play with all my stuff when you stayed over last week. I thought we were best friends. Why are you being so mean?"

Jess sighed. "OK, Lauren," she said. "Let's go."

Amber looked round at the rest of her friends; they were all as shocked as she was. The Jess they knew was usually so tough and always put Rose first, and yet here she was giving in to her pushy friend.

"Cool!" laughed Lauren. Before Jess could stop her, she'd grabbed Rose's reins and was trying to struggle into the saddle.

Amber didn't like this girl at all, but she was worried she might get hurt. "You need a crash cap," she called out.

Lauren spotted the hat that Jess had left on the fence while she groomed Rose. She jumped down, jammed it on her head, then turned to Jess, grinning. "Don't just stand there, give me a leg up," she ordered.

Looking embarrassed, Jess shoved her friend up into the saddle. Lauren snatched the reins, pulling hard on Rose's sensitive mouth. The gentle little Connemara whinnied and rolled her eyes nervously.

Jess stepped forward. "Don't do that, Lauren," she said quickly. "*Please.*"

Lauren tossed her head. "Oooh, aren't you little Miss Bossy Boots today?" she said in a mocking voice. "You think you're brilliant when you're at the stables, don't you?"

Jess said nothing and started to lead Rose away, but just at that moment Vicki walked across the yard and saw Lauren shouting and waving Rose's reins in the air. Her lovely grey eyes opened wide in surprise. "Where do you think you're taking Rose?" she called out.

29

Jess stopped dead in her tracks and blushed bright red. "Umm . . . I was just giving Lauren a quick ride," she muttered awkwardly.

Vicki shot across the yard and took hold of Rose's bridle. "Rose is going nowhere. She's worked hard all morning and I'm surprised that you expect more of her right now, Jess," she snapped. She glanced up at Lauren. "Get down, now," she said firmly.

The girls watched open-mouthed with shock as Lauren shook her head and grinned. "Sorry, don't know how to," she said, half joking.

Vicki did not look pleased. Her eyes flashed dangerously; it was a warning signal the girls knew well, and nobody in their right mind would mess with her now. Amber was secretly quite pleased. Maybe being told off by Vicki would stop Lauren behaving like such a know-it-all. Lauren didn't even seem to notice though. She sat astride Rose with a smug grin on her face. In one quick move Vicki, who was much stronger than she looked, reached up, lifted Lauren out of the saddle and plonked her down on the ground. She turned to Jess, who was now looking pale and nervous.

"Turn Rose out immediately or you won't be looking after her for very much longer," she told her, then walked off without looking back.

★

When the lessons were finished, the girls usually had fun, sharing their lunch boxes in the tack room, but this afternoon was different. Instead of laughing and messing around, they were all quiet, and poor Cara was so nervous she could barely eat.

Lauren totally made up for their silence though: she talked non-stop about how many boyfriends she had and how many parties she'd been to, then she asked the girls if any of them had boyfriends. Amber blushed and looked at the floor. She hated show-off conversations like this. Cara just sat with her mouth open in shock – Lauren might as well have asked her if she'd ever kissed an elephant!

"N-n-no, I've never had a boyfriend!" Cara blurted out.

By this time Amber was getting seriously fed up with Lauren and her one-way conversation. It was making everyone feel awkward.

"Boyfriends are a waste of time. I'd rather have ponies any day!" she said boldly. All the girls, except for Jess, nodded in agreement with Amber, but Lauren was not impressed.

"What a bunch of babies your friends are, Jess!" she laughed. Still smiling to herself, she started to help herself to a slice of cake from Sam's lunch box and some grapes from Jess's, then reached over to grab some of Mel's crisps.

Mel wasn't afraid to speak her mind to anybody and was really cross. "You could ask first," she said sharply. "You don't need to be rude."

Lauren grinned and flashed her dazzling white teeth as if Mel had just said something really friendly. "Chill out! Jess told me you all mucked in and shared stuff round," she said.

"We do – but you haven't brought anything to share with *us*!" Mel pointed out.

Lauren tossed her highlighted hair and turned to Jess. "I wish you'd mentioned how uptight your friends are," she said with a disappointed sigh. "I would've found a better riding school if I'd known."

Jess seemed to have lost her tongue: she shrugged and looked at the floor. Mel looked like she was ready to punch Lauren; the other girls were just shocked.

Sam tried to break the tense atmosphere by changing the subject. She picked up the newspaper that Amber had left on the tackroom table the week before. "Hey, girls. How you going with your sponsors?" she asked.

Amber didn't want to say that since last Saturday, when she'd heard Lauren would be coming to the stables, she'd hardly been able to think of anything else, so she shrugged and said, "It's been such a busy week I forgot all about it."

"I didn't," said Cara, chewing her nails like she always did when she was nervous. "I'm still a bit scared that they might make everybody do the high jumps."

"Honestly, Car, they won't," said Mel, putting an arm round her. "It doesn't work like that. You either do the ride with the high jumps or one with lower jumps."

Lauren, who hated not being the centre of attention, interrupted Mel. "What's this?" she demanded.

"It's a sponsored ride," Jess told her.

"What's that?" Lauren asked, "It sounds quite cool." And again Jess carefully explained.

All the girls were sick of Lauren taking over their conversation so Mel changed the subject again. "Shall we ask Darcy" she asked.

"Good idea, Mel," said Cara. "Darcy's wicked."

Lauren interrupted *again*. "So who am I gonna ride?" she demanded.

Her question puzzled them all. Lauren couldn't even ride yet, but here she was expecting to enter the sponsored jump!

"You have to learn to ride first," Sam said.

Lauren shrugged as if riding was

something she could do in her sleep. "So, Jess'll give me a couple of lessons on Rose and I'll be fine," she said.

Amber couldn't believe what this stupid girl was saying. The sponsored ride was in a week's time. It had taken her nearly three weeks of really hard work to learn how to even trot, let alone jump! Lauren must think that either she was some sort of genius, or that Jess was a miracle worker.

"You haven't even got a pony to ride!" Mel pointed out.

Again Lauren just shrugged and grinned. "Maybe Vicki will lend me one," she said cheerfully.

Amber saw Mel's amazed expression and she knew that they were both thinking the same thing. Did nothing bother Jess's big-headed friend?

Chapter 3

The next morning, while the yard girls and Darcy were cleaning their tack, Jess told them that Lauren had asked Vicki if she would give her some riding lessons during the week.

"Her parents must have quite a bit of money if they can afford to buy her lessons just like that," Amber said snidely.

Jess was rubbing saddle soap into Rose's bridle. "Lauren's not rich like the snooty livery girls," she said quickly.

Darcy looked up from the saddle she was polishing. "Hey, mind what you say about livery girls," she said in a jokey voice.

Amber could
tell she was a
bit annoyed
though. She
was standing
next to
Darcy, so she
gave her a
dig in the ribs
with her elbow to
try and lighten the
mood. "Of course, you're a nice livery girl,"
she said with a giggle.

Cara looked puzzled. "So how's she going
to pay for her riding lessons, if her parents
aren't dead rich?" she asked.

Jess smiled at her. "Lauren can get
anything she wants out of her dad; she just
twists him round her little finger," she replied,
as though she thought this was a brilliant
thing to be able to do.

Sam grinned. "Sounds just like Henrietta Snooty Knickers – she never stops bossing her dad about!" she joked. "Maybe they'll be friends."

The tack-room door suddenly swung open and banged against the wall. Treasure and Hunt had been sleeping on an old rug under the table but the noise woke them and they started to bark.

"Talk of the devil," Mel muttered.

In walked Henrietta and Camilla. "What are those mongrels doing in here?" Henrietta screwed up her nose as she looked at the puppies.

"Treasure and Hunt live here: they can go anywhere they want," Mel snapped.

"If they go anywhere near my tack, I'll kick them right out the door," Henrietta threatened.

Amber couldn't stand cruelty of any kind and she glared at her. "If you do that, I'll

40

report you to the RSPCA," she warned.

The horrible livery girls grabbed their tack boxes and were just about to storm off when Henrietta spotted Amber's newspaper lying open on the table.

"Please don't tell me you lot are doing the sponsored ride too," she said.

Sam's eyes flashed. "It's open to everyone," she pointed out.

Amber nodded. "The more the merrier as far as the organizers are concerned."

Henrietta tossed her well-cut blonde bob and looked at the girls as if they were something disgusting on the bottom of her shoe. "Camilla and I will be going for the double-tier rosette: it's only for the advanced riders who can manage the red jumps  on the course," she said snootily.

"Jess, Sam and Mel are going for the double-tier rosette too," Amber said quickly.

Camilla smiled mockingly. "I hope their old ponies are up to it – you don't get sponsored for a refused jump, you know," she said.

Mel's dark eyes glinted dangerously and she moved closer to Henrietta and Camilla. "You won't find Candy refusing any jumps," she snapped.

Henrietta cracked her riding whip against her expensive new jodhpurs. "I already know how much money I'm going to raise. Daddy's sponsoring me for five hundred pounds," she boasted.

Camilla looked down her long nose. "I couldn't bear to go grovelling around asking people for money," she said.

Henrietta pulled a face, as if the very thought made her feel sick. "So nasty to have to mix with low-life!" she said. Then, turning on her heel, she flounced off, with Camilla running along behind her.

Darcy was the first to speak. "Those two idiots are *so* on another planet," she seethed.

"I wish!" Sam joked. "Then we'd never have to see their moody faces again."

Lauren had two riding lessons with Vicki after school that week, and the girls were surprised at how quickly she *did* pick up the basics. She rode Bubbles, Vicki's dark bay Dartmoor pony who was semi-retired.

"He's old but willing, so make sure you treat him kindly," Vicki said.

In between the lessons Jess had asked Vicki if Lauren could trot round the field on Rose and try a few low jumps.

Vicki looked surprised. "Lauren's in danger of learning to run before she can walk," she said sharply. "I thought you were more sensible than this, Jess. You shouldn't encourage her."

Jess blushed. "She's hoping to do the sponsored ride with us on Saturday. I was just going to set up a few low jumps to give her some practice," she explained quickly.

Vicki slowly nodded her head. "OK, but be

really careful, and she has to do the stepping poles first," she said.

So Lauren borrowed Rose and rode in the outdoor school. First she trotted, then she did some work with the poles, which Jess laid on the ground about a yard apart.

"All you have to do is trot over the poles, keeping a nice steady rhythm, without falling off," Jess explained.

Lauren trotted over the poles without any accidents, then tossed her head and said impatiently, "Come on, Jess, this is kid's stuff."

Scared of getting another mouthful from Vicki, Jess insisted that Lauren did some more work on the poles, but then, as usual, she gave in to her and set up a few low jumps, no more than a foot high.

Watched by Jess and the girls, Lauren took her first jump. Amber wanted to say that Rose was an experienced little jumper, and she could have done the jump with her eyes shut, but big-headed Lauren thought it was all down to her. As she finished the novice course without any mistakes, she screamed excitedly, "Easy-peasy!"

Scared by Lauren's loud voice, Rose tossed her head and whinnied nervously.

"Stop being stupid, Pony!" Lauren shouted.

Jess looked shocked, and for the first time the girls heard her speak sharply to her friend.

"Rose *isn't* being stupid, she's just sensitive to loud noises," she said quickly. "Lots of ponies are."

Lauren clapped her heels into Rose's side. "I'm going round again," she announced.

Jess shook her head. "She's probably had enough for today," she said firmly.

Lauren dismounted sulkily, then threw the reins at Jess. "You can keep your lazy nag. Now that I can ride, I'm going to ask Vicki if I can try one of the livelier ponies. No offence, guys, but Stella and Taffy are pretty boring too."

Amber and Cara looked shocked. "Candy and Beanz are right up my street though!" Lauren added, turning to grin at Mel and Sam.

★

In the privacy of the stables, Mel, Sam, and Cara were fuming over what Lauren had said. But Amber just felt like crying. Jess was completely different now this horrible girl was around.

"How dare she think she can ride Candy!" Mel fumed.

Sam always managed to see the funny side of things. "Lauren's been riding for nearly a week now – maybe it's time for the Badminton horse trials!" she giggled. "She probably thinks she could do it!"

At that, Amber giggled too. "I hope she does ride Beanz – he'd buck her into another country!"

Cara wasn't smiling though, and she looked worried as she nibbled nervously at her fingernails. "Everything's changed since Lauren arrived," she said sadly.

Amber nodded. She was pleased that she

wasn't the only one who thought so. She could hardly believe that her best friend was being bossed around by a big-headed know-it-all who loved the sound of her own voice so much.

Mel tossed her dark black curls and said what they were all thinking: "It's all Jess's fault for bringing Lauren here in the first place!"

★

Getting enough sponsors for the race took the girls' minds off Lauren for a few days. They nagged their family and school friends, their neighbours and teachers; Amber even got the owners of one of the local shops to back her. They put all their sponsor forms on the old wooden table in the tack room and added up the grand total.

"If everybody coughs up we could make over two hundred quid between us," Sam said excitedly.

Cara looked worried again. "That's if we manage to do all the jumps on the course," she said.

Amber gave her a comforting pat on the arm. "You know better than anybody that Taffy can do that course with his eyes closed," she said.

Cheeky Sam joked, "That's if Lauren's not borrowed him!"

Cara's blue eyes flashed and her face went pink. "She'd better not even try," she cried.

The girls quickly stopped talking when Lauren and Jess walked in. The pair of them had been spending lots of time together, driving to the yard in Lauren's mum's car, sneaking off to Rose's stable to chat in secret, eating lunch together. They never invited Amber and it hurt her a lot.

"We've just been going though the rules for the sponsored ride," Lauren said in a loud, bossy voice.

Amber blinked in surprise. From the confident way Lauren talked, anybody would have thought she'd been riding for years.

Jess didn't seem to notice Lauren's bad manners. "Did you know we have to ride in groups of three?" she asked them.

"Oh, I didn't see that," said Amber.

Mel held up three fingers. "Me, Darcy and Sam are doing the high red jumps so we could be in one group," she suggested.

Amber was busy counting on her fingers too. "That leaves me, Jess and Cara," she said.

Lauren loudly interrupted her. "*I'm* riding with Jess," she said.

The girls stared at each other. There were six of them including Darcy. She wasn't there at the moment but she was a good jumper and would definitely want to do the high red jumps. If Lauren rode, that would take their number up to seven, which meant that somebody would be left out of the ride. They all turned to Jess, hoping that she would say something to Lauren, but she didn't.

Amber's dark eyes flashed angrily. Not only had Lauren taken over her best friend, she was now taking over the sponsored ride too! Determined to ignore Lauren, Amber looked straight at Jess. "So who's in your group then?" she demanded.

Lauren didn't give Jess the chance to answer. "Me, Jess and . . . Cara, I suppose," she said. "Jess said you're not as good since you broke your arm and we don't want you holding us back."

Amber struggled to hold back her tears. She hoped that Jess hadn't made this decision and that it was all down to Lauren. But Jess had let her get away with it and that hurt most of all. She didn't know what to say, but Mel leaped to her defence.

"So who's Amber with?" she demanded.

Lauren shrugged. "Dunno," she said in a voice that meant *And I don't care either.*

Amber'd had enough; she burst into tears and ran sobbing out of the tack room.

Cara and Sam immediately ran after her, but Mel held back. She glared at Jess, who was blushing with shame.

"You cow! How could you do this to Amber when it was her idea in the first place?" she shouted. "She's supposed to be your best friend." Then she stormed angrily out of the tack room, leaving Jess looking really miserable but Lauren with a big smile on her face.

The problem of the groups was solved a few minutes later when Darcy turned up and heard what had happened.

"Don't worry," she said. "I'm not going to do the sponsored ride. Amber can have my place."

Sam and Mel smiled with relief. "You can ride with us then," Sam said to Amber.

But Cara shook her head. "No way, it should be me who doesn't do it, Darcy. You and Amber are miles better and you'll raise more money for the school."

Amber wiped her tear-stained face.

"That's so sweet, Car, but I don't really feel like doing it now anyway, and you'll enjoy it when you're there. You do it."

"No," Darcy said. "I've got an audition for the school choir. I don't want to do it, but my mum's on my case. I guess if I do the audition I'll keep her happy and you guys can all do the sponsored jump."

"Well, I don't really even want to be in the same room as Jess and her horrible new friend at the moment, but I won't let you guys down and it would be good to raise some money, so OK," Amber said.

Sam, Amber and Cara looked at each other — they knew it would take Amber a long time to get over Jess dumping her like this. Would the girls ever make up?

Chapter 4

The following day the girls were all worried about Bubbles: Lauren was riding him in a practice jump session in the outdoor school.

Amber had a real understanding of ponies and their needs and she was very concerned. "He's not used to such rough treatment," she said crossly, watching Lauren saw at his mouth with the reins.

But within ten minutes Lauren was bored with Bubbles anyway. "He's *soooooo* slow," she grumbled to Jess.

"He's lovely, just a bit stiff in the joints," Jess replied.

"He's boring!" Lauren snapped. She gave

Bubbles a thump in the ribs with her heels. "Come on, lazy bones!" she yelled at him.

Amber glared at Jess, wishing she'd say something to her cruel friend, but she didn't, so she said something herself. "Treat him gently, Lauren," she snapped.

Lauren looked daggers at Amber but didn't say anything back.

When Vicki arrived to give them some coaching, she left Amber, Mel and Sam to practise their advanced jumping and set up a simple course of low jumps for Jess, Cara and Lauren.

"They look too high for me!" Cara said nervously.

Vicki smiled. "Imagine it's the sponsored ride and you'll get a pound for every jump you do," she said encouragingly.

Jess popped over the jumps easily and so did Cara, even though she'd been so worried. Lauren did well considering she was only a learner but she obviously hated taking advice.

"You're doing OK, Lauren, but you have to turn your feet in," Vicki told her. "At the moment they're sticking out and you look very awkward."

Lauren scowled and her face went bright red. From Jess's alarmed expression it was clear that she was worried that Lauren might give Vicki a mouthful. Luckily she didn't and the coaching continued. Bubbles was patient with Lauren for a while, but after about half an hour he'd had enough and refused a jump.

Instead of encouraging him with a pat and a kind word, Lauren lost her temper. "Move!" she screamed. There was no way

Bubbles was going to move for such a rude rider and he stamped his feet and shook his head. Then, to everybody's horror, Lauren laid into him with her riding whip.

Quick as a flash, Vicki grabbed the reins from her. "Get down immediately!" she said in a steely voice.

Lauren dismounted and looked at Vicki but didn't even try to apologize. Jess looked really shocked. This was obviously the first time she'd seen what her wonderful new friend was really like.

Vicki glared at Lauren. "After that little display, you certainly won't be riding any of my ponies on the sponsored ride, or ever again," she said icily.

Lauren shrugged, and walked away without saying a word.

When the coaching session was over and the girls had untacked their ponies and turned them out into the meadow, Jess went looking for Lauren.

"I hope she's gone home and never comes back," Amber seethed.

Mel pulled a funny face. "We should be so lucky!" she muttered.

Five minutes later, when Amber was crossing the yard, she was gobsmacked to see Lauren in President's stable. Seeing her deep in conversation with the snooty livery girls, Amber slowed her steps so that she could listen to what they were saying.

"I'm sick to death of Jess telling me what to do," Lauren complained.

"She thinks she knows everything about riding when in fact she hardly knows one end of a pony from the other," Henrietta scoffed.

"I've noticed," said Lauren. "At school she makes out she knows everything about ponies, but she's just a show-off, I reckon. Rose is well boring and that Bubbles is totally useless — he wouldn't even do the baby jumps."

The livery girls laughed. "It's about time Vicki packed him off to the knacker's yard," Henrietta said with a sneer in her voice. "It's the best place for him."

Lauren's reply made Amber gasp. "Too right — he'd be better off dead!" she laughed.

Amber hurried away. She was totally disgusted by what she'd just heard Lauren say. She went to find a quiet spot where she could think. Should she tell Jess what she'd overheard? She really wanted to, but she didn't know if Jess would believe her or if she'd just think that Amber was jealous and slagging Lauren off for the sake of it.

With her head whirling, Amber made for the tack room, where she hoped to find Sam, Darcy, Cara and Mel so she could ask them what they thought. They were all in the tack room polishing their tack, but to Amber's disappointment Lauren was there too, pleading with Jess.

"I'm *so* sorry, Jess, I should never have behaved like that. I just got over-excited," Lauren said in a whiny, little-girl voice.

Amber gasped. What an act she was putting on!

"I totally understand why Vicki's mad at me — I should never have treated Bubbles like that," Lauren went on as she pretended to wipe away a tear. "I just panicked when he wouldn't jump. You're my best friend, Jess. You know I'm not cruel."

Seeing Lauren's sad face, Jess quickly gave her a big hug. "Everything's fine. We've all panicked before. Everyone just reacts differently. Come on, let's go and apologize to Vicki right away," she said.

They walked out of the tack room arm in arm, leaving the other five girls open-mouthed with amazement.

"Wow! I can't believe Jess has fallen for it again!" Amber gasped.

While Jess and Lauren were out the way, she quickly told her friends what she'd overheard Lauren saying in President's stable.

Mel couldn't believe her ears. "She's sucking up to Snooty Knickers!" she cried in horror. "I didn't like her before but now I can't stand her!"

"It looked like she was getting on with her and Camilla like a house on fire," Amber went on.

Cara looked concerned. "I can't believe Lauren said such horrible things about Bubbles."

"I can! She's so two-faced," Darcy said.

Sam ran a hand through her ginger hair. "She's all sweet to Jess's face, then behind her back she's slagging her off," she fumed.

Amber's dark eyes were thoughtful. She didn't want her friend to get hurt, even if she was being a bit off at the moment. "We really should tell Jess," she said.

Darcy shook her head. "She'd never believe us. She'd probably think we were just being horrible," she said. "It's like Lauren's put a spell on her or something."

The rest of the girls agreed.

"So what do we do — sit back and do nothing until Jess finds out and gets really upset?" Mel fumed.

Cara nervously chewed her fingernails. "It's really horrible. But there's not much else we can do," she said.

Amber sighed. "With a bit of luck Jess will soon find out for herself what a user Lauren is," she said.

Lauren and Jess managed to persuade Vicki
to let Lauren have another go on Bubbles,
but after that Lauren seemed to want to
spend more and more time on the livery side
of the yard with Henrietta and Camilla, and
less and less with Jess. And soon she was even
speaking like them. As Sam, Cara, Mel and
Amber were helping at the yard one evening
after school, Sam, who was a good mimic,
did a wicked impression of Lauren.

"Yah, yah, super, smashing, yah!" she
mocked.

Amber, Cara and Mel burst out laughing,
but stopped immediately when they saw Jess
turn the corner. They could see she was upset
and the last thing they wanted to do was
make her feel even worse.

"Why does Lauren like being with
Henrietta and Camilla so much?" she blurted
out straight away. "They're horrible."

Mel shrugged. "Maybe she likes the smell of money," she said.

Jess shook her head, looking puzzled. "She wasn't like that before. She's always been so nice."

The others didn't try to argue.

"But I even saw her sucking up to Henrietta's horrible grumpy dad when he dropped her off earlier," Jess continued.

Sam tried to make a joke of it. "That's pretty desperate," she laughed.

Amber kept her mouth shut. She didn't want to stir and make Jess go off her even more, but she was convinced that Lauren was after something only the rich girls could give her.

★

Lauren finally showed up in Rose's stable wearing a big plastic smile and carrying a big plastic bag. Amber, who was mucking out Stella's stable next door, heard her arrive.

"Take a look at all this," she said as she
tipped the bag onto the clean straw bed that
Jess had just spread out for Rose.

Jess couldn't believe her eyes when she saw
a nearly new pair of jodhpurs, a hacking
jacket, a smart white shirt and a tie that even
had a little gold pony pin stuck to it. "Where
did that lot come from?" she gasped.

Lauren smirked. "Henrietta's grown out of
them," she said.

Jess blushed. She'd look well shabby on the sponsored ride now, compared to Lauren in her posh cast-offs.

"I don't know how you can have anything to do with Henrietta," she said angrily. "She's a horrible snob."

Lauren laughed at Jess's red face. "Oooh, moody, moody! You're only saying that because you're jealous of her money and embarrassed that your mum works at the supermarket," she sneered.

Jess glared at Lauren's smug face. "I am *not* jealous. Henrietta's mean and nasty. It's got nothing to do with money," she shouted indignantly.

Lauren shrugged and replied in a snooty voice that sounded exactly like the livery girls', "Henrietta's cool, and President is gorgeous – he's got so much more class than the old nags you and your silly mates ride."

Amber caught her breath at Lauren's cruel

remarks. But she smiled to herself as Jess hit back.

"Our ponies were good enough for you last week," she snapped.

"Yeah, well, now I know better, don't I? Henrietta and Camilla are class and so are their ponies!"

Before Jess could say another word, Lauren picked the clothes up off the floor and stomped out of the stable. From Stella's half-open stable door Amber saw her run across the yard to President's stable, where Henrietta and Camilla were waiting for her.

Chapter 5

Amber hurried into Rose's stable, where she found Jess crying her eyes out.

"Did you hear what Lauren just said?" Jess asked as she tried to wipe her eyes on her sleeve.

Amber nodded and gave her friend a hug. "She was yelling so much I reckon everybody heard," she replied.

"She's not like that at school. She used to be really nice," Jess said miserably. "She's really popular and I was well pleased when she wanted to be my friend and invited me to her sleepover and stuff."

Amber looked at her friend's tear-stained face and decided that Lauren could never have been really nice and it was time to spill the beans. "I heard Lauren with Camilla and Henrietta a couple of days ago slagging off us and the ponies," she said. "I don't think she's as nice as you thought." She didn't tell Jess what she'd heard Lauren say about her. She knew it would only upset her more.

Jess's green eyes flashed angrily. "I wish I'd never brought her here," she seethed.

★

As Amber comforted Jess on one side of the

yard, Camilla was making a plan on the other side. She was getting annoyed with this common new girl, Lauren, who thought she was just as good as her and Henrietta. Who did she think she was, sucking up to Hen and making Camilla feel left out?

Camilla had never wanted to do the sponsored ride right from the start. Jumping wasn't her thing, and Cleo went crazy when she was with a crowd of ponies, so now she'd come up with a plan to get out of the stupid sponsored ride and get rid of Lauren.

After her row with Jess, Lauren had come running into President's stable with a smirk on her face just as Camilla's mobile rang. "I've just told that pathetic Jess exactly what I think of her," Lauren bragged.

Henrietta's mean little eyes lit up – the more she got to know Lauren the more she liked her.

Lauren tossed her head and carried on

showing off. "I told her President was in a totally different class to their old nags," she boasted.

Behind their backs Camilla pretended to talk to her mother on the phone. "No, Mum, I can't do that. It's the day of the sponsored ride — I can't let Hen down," she said dramatically.

At the sound of her name Henrietta turned sharply to Camilla, who had switched off her phone and was looking upset.

"You'll never believe what Mummy's gone and done," she exclaimed.

Henrietta shrugged impatiently. "Tell me," she snapped.

"She's taking me school uniform shopping tomorrow," Camilla said.

Henrietta glared at her. She, Camilla and a snooty girl from their posh school were riding as a group the next day. "We won't be able to do the sponsored ride if you're not with us," she said angrily.

Camilla pretended to look sad. "I'm sorry, Hen, but once Mummy's made her mind up, there's nothing that will change it," she said quietly.

Catching Henrietta's eye, she went on deliberately, "I'll happily lend Cleo to anybody who fancies riding her though . . ."

Henrietta's furious expression gradually faded, to be replaced by a smile. "I think I know just the person," she whispered with a smirk. She did quite like Lauren, and she loved the way she sucked up to her, but she was a bit common really, and Henrietta knew she'd really struggle with Cleo. It might be fun to watch!

★

The following morning Jess and Amber arrived at the yard at the crack of dawn. This was the last day of their week on livery duty so they needed to muck out President's and Cleopatra's stables and groom them ready for the sponsored ride. Then they'd have to rush and do the same for Rose and Stella.

Jess wasn't her usual self at all. "I'm dreading seeing Lauren," she finally said to Amber. "I've been such an idiot. I really wish she wasn't in our group."

Amber nodded in complete agreement. "But it's too late to change anything — we're stuck with her for the sponsored ride," she pointed out.

Jess sighed heavily. "How did I get myself into this mess?" she said. "I thought she was brilliant and I just wanted her to like me."

Amber gave her a hug. "Try not to think about Lauren; think about the money you'll raise for the special needs school instead," she said cheerily.

At the sound of the girls' voices, President popped his head over the half-open stable door and whinnied loudly.

"Hello, gorgeous boy," Amber called out to him. Stroking his velvety dark muzzle, she led him out into the yard, where she tied him up and started to brush him down.

Jess groomed Cleo, who was in a bad mood as usual and kept trying to bite her. She turned to Amber and shook her head. "This pony is mad!" she grumbled. "And just as snooty as her owner!"

Amber nodded. "It's not a nice thing to say about a poor pony but I think you could be right. She's a perfect match for Camilla!" she said with a laugh.

When they'd finished mucking out, feeding and grooming the livery ponies, Jess and Amber ran back across the yard and started to groom Stella and Rose.

The other girls were all busy with their ponies, but they could see that Jess was looking over her shoulder all the time.

"Where's Lauren?" she fretted. "We've got

to leave in a few minutes and she hasn't even started to tack up Bubbles yet."

Mel looked annoyed. "We don't want to be late for the sponsored ride just because Lauren can't get her act together," she said.

Suddenly a vehicle swung into the yard: it was Mr Reece-Thomas's flashy silver four-wheel drive. The girls could see Henrietta sitting in the front next to her dad, but there was also somebody in the back. As the car sped by, they all gasped out loud. Sitting in the back seat was not Camilla but Lauren!

Amber looked at Jess's shocked face. "I think it's time to find out what Lauren's up to," she said firmly.

★

When Jess opened President's stable door, Henrietta scowled at her. "Who invited you in here?" she snapped, looking at her like she was scum.

Jess ignored her and turned to Lauren, who looked really smart in Henrietta's old clothes. "We're all waiting for you," she said sharply. "We need to leave in a few minutes. Bubbles is waiting to be tacked up."

Lauren gave her a cold hard stare. "Well, you're wasting your time – I'm riding with Henrietta now," she told her.

Jess blinked in amazement. "I thought you were riding in *our* group?"

Lauren shook her highlighted hair. "Sorry, I've had a better offer," she replied.

Amber couldn't take any more. Raging,

she joined Jess in the stable, where she glared at Lauren. "Who are you riding then?" she demanded.

Lauren laughed. "Not knackered old Bubbles, that's for sure."

Henrietta smirked and answered for Lauren. "She's riding Cleo," she said.

Jess went pale. "Are you out of your mind? Cleo's vicious!" she cried. "Henrietta, you know that."

"You're just jealous, as usual!" Lauren sneered.

Amber tried to warn Lauren too. "Cleo's bad enough with an experienced rider but with a novice like you—" she started to say.

Lauren's eyes nearly popped out of her head. "I am *not* a novice rider!" she screamed at them.

Jess grabbed Lauren's arm and tried to reason with her. "Listen! It's daft to even think of taking on Cleo – honestly, Lauren."

Henrietta gave her a shove. "Get out of my stable," she said in a threatening voice.

Lauren smirked. "I hope you've groomed Cleo well, Jess. I want her looking her best for the sponsored ride," she said snootily.

Jess looked daggers at her. "You're scheming and two-faced!" she fumed.

★

In Rose's stable, surrounded by her friends, Jess was cross with herself.

"I've ruined our chances for the sponsored ride!" she cried. "I'm such an idiot."

Seeing Jess so upset made all the girls forget how annoyed they'd been with her before. Like all good friends, they just wanted to make everything better again. Cara gave

Jess her hankie to blow her nose on, Mel
offered her a piece of chewing gum and Sam
typically cracked a joke.

"Think positive, Jess: now it's Henrietta
who's getting all the earache!"

The girls were disappointed that only three
of them would be able to ride now; they were
just starting to decide who it should be when
Darcy saved the day again. She surprised
them all by walking into Rose's stable with a
grin on her face.

"I'm not going to the choir thing now," she announced. "Is there room for me on a team?"

The girls threw themselves on Darcy and smothered her with hugs and kisses. Jess squeezed her so hard she took her breath away.

"You star!"

Cara giggled happily. "What made you change your mind?" she asked.

Darcy pulled a face. "Well, I wanted to do the ride really, but there were too many of us and I had the choir thing so it was easier for me to say I couldn't come. But then I heard what Lauren said to Jess while I was grooming Duke. I was so angry I wanted to slap her face, but I thought of another way of getting back at Miss Two Faces instead," she said with a wicked smile. "I'm not going to let her ruin it for all of us. And I can't wait to see how she handles Cleo."

"What will your mum say about the choir though?" asked Cara. "I thought she wanted you to join."

"She did till she heard me practising last night. I think she knows now I'm better with ponies than I am at singing!"

Everyone laughed. Amber grinned at Jess, who smiled back.

"Come on," said Amber. "We'd better get a move on or we'll never get there on time!"

Chapter 6

They arrived at the course ten minutes before the jumping was due to start. Darcy hadn't registered yet, so she legged it across to the officials' tent, where she was given an entry number like the rest of the girls. Because of the sudden change of plan, she hadn't had any time to find sponsors, but she quickly rang home on her mobile and her parents each promised twenty pounds if she completed the course.

On the short ride over, the girls had sorted out their groups again. Darcy would join Mel and Sam and do the red jumps as they'd planned in the first place, and Amber would do the low jumps with Jess and Cara.

"You're in the same group you would have been in if I hadn't been brainwashed by Lauren," Jess said apologetically to Amber. "I'm so sorry. I feel like a total cow."

"I don't care, babe – I'm just happy that we're friends again," Amber said with a big smile. And she meant it.

Darcy joined her friends just as Henrietta's posh horsebox trundled onto the course.

"They're here!" Amber cried.

Mr Reece-Thomas, who was even more red in the face than normal, jumped out of his flashy car, followed by Henrietta and Lauren, who stood by and lazily watched him struggle with the heavy trailer door. When he'd lowered it to the ground, Henrietta went up the ramp; a few minutes later she reappeared leading President, whose ears were pricked with excitement. Seeing Jess and her friends staring at her, Lauren smirked and swaggered up the ramp.

The watching girls held their breath – they all knew how difficult Cleopatra was to box and un-box.

Amber shook her head when she heard the wild, headstrong pony squealing and kicking the partition door. "If Lauren survives an hour on Cleo it'll be a miracle," she said. Secretly, though, she was really quite worried that Lauren might get hurt.

There was no time to walk the course, but that didn't matter – they weren't racing against the clock. Groups were setting off and doing the jumps in their own time, chatting to each other as they went round.

When Cara saw how low the green jumps were, she smiled with relief. "They're just right for me," she said happily.

Mel grinned too when she saw the high red jumps. "And they're so perfect for me," she laughed excitedly.

There was a steward at every jump

keeping a record of the riders who'd jumped. The atmosphere was chilled out and everybody seemed to be in a good mood.

Amber, Jess and Cara popped over the first couple of jumps easily, then met Vicki, who was acting as the steward at the third jump.

Vicki had ridden over on Jelly, who was tied to a nearby fence enjoying his day out. The three girls spent some time fussing over Jelly, who was as gorgeous as his owner, then trotted over to join the queue of excited boys and girls who were waiting to jump over the low log.

Amber waved across at Vicki, but strangely, she didn't wave back at her. Her stunning silver grey eyes were wide open and she was staring past them at something, with a horrified expression on her tanned face.

Cara noticed that Amber was following her gaze. "What's the matter with Vicki?" she gasped.

Seconds later they knew exactly what the matter was. There was a totally out-of-control rider pounding up the bank on a galloping pony. And heading straight towards them!

"Get out of the way!" Vicki screamed at the top of her voice.

Some of the competitors managed to move to the side but some weren't as quick, and now they were right in the path of the crazed pony. Amber had the keenest eyesight and she gasped as she recognized the rider.

"Oh, my God – it's Lauren!" she cried, her heart pounding.

Screaming her head off, her reins flying loose, Lauren was hanging onto Cleo's long mane with all her strength. The crazy pony flashed by, scaring loads of competitors as she passed. Some of the ponies bolted and scattered in all directions, and a few of the younger riders fell off, only just escaping being trampled by Cleopatra's thundering hooves. Covered in sweat, with the whites of her eyes showing, Cleo galloped up over a low hill and out of sight.

The girls were so shocked they couldn't even speak. Luckily Vicki took charge. She sprinted over and quickly untied Jelly. As she mounted up, she called out to the girls, "There's a main road at the bottom of that hill – if I don't stop Cleo, they could both be killed!"

Amber, Jess and Cara leaped into action. They pounded up the hill after Vicki. They gasped as they reached the summit and saw Vicki closing in on Cleo, but the pony didn't look like she was going to slow down even though the main road was just ahead.

Cara hid her face in her hands. "Lauren's going to die!" she wailed.

Jess shook her head as if she couldn't believe what she was seeing. "Why doesn't she just throw herself off?" she cried.

"She could break her neck if she did that," Amber muttered.

Holding their breath, the girls watched

Jelly come up alongside Cleo. They all knew Vicki was an amazing horsewoman but they didn't know until that moment how brave she was too. Gripping Jelly with her legs, she swung over and grabbed Cleopatra's flying reins; she tugged at them with all her might.

"Whoa, girl, *whoa*," she cried.

Hearing a strong voice and feeling a firm hand on her reins, Cleo began to slow down. Finally she came to a shuddering halt, traffic rushing by on the main road only metres in front of her, and Lauren slid to the ground.

Watching from the top of the hill, Amber, Jess and Cara slumped forwards in their saddles with relief.

"Vicki's saved Lauren's life," Jess said weakly.

Amber shook her head in amazement. "What a hero!" she gasped.

The girls cantered down the hill to join Vicki. She was holding firmly onto Cleo, who was foaming at the mouth and shaking all over.

"Ssh, girl, you're OK. Everything's all right," Vicki said in a low voice that started to calm Cleo straight away.

As the girls dismounted, she held up a warning hand. "Ssh, keep it down – Cleo's in shock," she told them.

Lauren was sitting on the ground, crying hysterically. She stopped to give Vicki a dirty look. "What about me? I'm in shock too," she sobbed.

Vicki gave her a cold stare and said, "Who's to blame for that?"

Lauren jumped to her feet and, with everybody staring at her, screamed, "I am never ever going anywhere near a stinking mangy pony as long as I live!"

At the sound of her hysterical voice Cleopatra shied, but Vicki held her tight and steadied her. She turned  to look at Lauren. "I certainly hope not. You will definitely *never* ride any pony from *my* yard." Then, very clearly, she added, "I don't want to see you anywhere near my stables ever again."

Lauren scowled at them all, then stomped off up the hill. "You should shoot that mental Cleopatra — and those stuck-up livery girls too!" she yelled as she went.

Vicki shrugged and smiled as Lauren disappeared out of sight. "I really hope that's the last we ever see of her," she said.

★

Vicki didn't want to take Cleo back through the crowded course so she walked her the short distance back to the stables. The three girls went too: Amber led Jelly, who kept nuzzling her in the back, Jess led both Stella and Rose, and Cara followed behind with Taffy. As they trudged along, Amber thought about the strange day they'd had. After Darcy turned up, she'd been so excited about the sponsored ride and she'd wanted to make loads of money for the special needs school. But her team had managed only two jumps, Lauren had nearly got herself killed, they'd abandoned the event, and here they all were, walking back to the stables. But most importantly, Amber had got her best friend back: she just couldn't stop smiling!

"You could say the sponsored ride was a total disaster then," Amber said, to try and cheer everybody up.

But Jess wasn't in the mood for joking. "It was a disaster from the moment Lauren got involved," she said honestly. "This is all my fault."

"We all make mistakes, hon," Vicki said softly, but then her eyes narrowed angrily. "Just wait till I get my hands on that stupid Camilla Worthington though – what on earth was she thinking, lending a pony like Cleopatra to a novice rider?"

Amber, Cara and Jess exchanged a knowing look. "I'm sure Henrietta had something to do with it as usual," Amber said.

★

By the time they got back to the yard, Cleo had totally calmed down. She didn't make a fuss when Vicki untacked her, and for once she didn't even try to bite while the girls brushed her down. She was snugly tucked up in her stable, which had a nice deep litter of straw, when Henrietta came back to the yard in her dad's fancy car with the horsebox attached. When Mr Reece-Thomas saw Jess and Amber coming out of the tack room, he yelled at them like they were servants.

"Take President to his stable!" he snapped.

Amber felt like giving the rude, bad-tempered man a mouthful, but she'd definitely had enough of arguments over the last couple of weeks! She said nothing, and turned to President: he looked worn out, and Amber felt really sorry for him.

"Come on, sweetheart. Let's get you a nice big supper," she said softly. The gentle Appaloosa nudged her arm affectionately and Amber's heart ached for him. She was sure nobody had said a nice word to him all day.

As the girls turned to lead President away, Henrietta scowled at Jess. "By the way, if you see that loser Lauren around, tell her she's pathetic – she can't even take a little joke," she snapped.

Jess smiled: this was a message she would enjoy delivering. "With pleasure," she said.

★

Darcy, Mel and Sam got back as the autumn

sun was almost gone; it looked like there might be rain. Sam waved excitedly when she saw the other three girls. "Where did you get to?" she asked.

"We made a hundred and fifty quid on the sponsored ride."

Amber burst out laughing. "Cool! We made six pounds!" she giggled.

As Darcy, Mel and Sam untacked their tired ponies, the others told them about their adventure.

"Cleo bolted at the second jump and stampeded through the crowd," Jess said.

Mel's dark eyes opened wide in amazement. "Did Lauren fall off?" she gasped.

Cara shook her head. "She just managed to hang on," she replied.

"Vicki went after her on Jelly and managed to stop Cleo just before she galloped out into the main road," Amber added, thinking again how amazing Vicki was.

Mel, Sam and Darcy gaped at them.

"Lauren could be dead if it wasn't for Vicki," Darcy said slowly.

Jess nodded her head seriously.

"What a stupid idiot!" Mel cried.

Amber grinned. "But the good news is, Lauren's given up riding for ever!" she giggled.

Sam punched the air and whooped with joy. "Yesss!" she said with a laugh. "That's the best news I've had all year!"

Amber smiled. "That seems to be everybody's opinion. Even Snooty Knickers!"

"With a bit of luck we won't see Lauren ever again," Mel said.

Cara looked at Jess and smiled nervously. "Poor Jess will have to see her every day at school, though," she pointed out.

Jess shook her head and grinned. "Now that I've seen the real Lauren, I'll never have anything to do with her again," she promised.

Amber grinned and gave Jess a big hug. "I'm so pleased to have my best friend back," she said.

THE END